Jacobson
Castle
Rainbow Dragons
Castle
Mare Occeanum

This book is dedicated to Besty Jacobson.

Merry Christmas 2011

With love from Dad

Introduction

I first introduced the world to the adventures of the rainbow dragons in 1987. After my son's birth in 2006, we have spent countless hours and adventures with the rainbow dragons.

At Besty's request, I am finally adding a new adventure to the saga.

I would also like to thank Emily Funk for the amazing cover art.

I would like to now formally invite you to save the Rainbow Dragons' Castle.

- Brad Jacobson

On a windswept October day as the leaves dance around the court yard, you stare past the castle's tower into the sky. In the distance a small speck on the horizon slowly grows in size as it flies toward you. As the sun's rays dance across its back, you have to shade your eyes as you are bathed in a prism of light. You strain your ears to gently hear "floop, floop, floop, floop" as gentle as a summer breeze. Then within moments, you have to lean forward to keep from being knocked over as the gusts from each flap create gale force winds and a deafening howl.

Suddenly the wind stops and the earth rumbles and shakes and as you gaze up, you are bathed in a rainbow and a smile from your good friend – RB, the rainbow dragon.

With his massive claw, he pats you on the head and says "It's wonderful to see you, Besty".

"Thank you RB, to what do I owe the honour of your visit today?" you reply.

"The rainbow dragons' castle is in great danger. When we built it with your forefather Jacob, we built it at the edge of a cliff facing the ocean in our homeland of

Norway because the lift provided by the wind makes it easy for us to take off. Now the cliff is unstable and the entire castle could fall into the ocean at any moment. When we built the castle, we promised to never let anyone but a son of Jacob into our castle. Due to our size, a dragon cannot enter beneath the castle to remove the ancient bolts that anchor the foundation to the cliff. Can you help us?"

If you would like to leave immediately to help the rainbow dragons turn to page 7

If you would like to wait and discuss the matter with your father turn to page 10

As you climb the massive dragon's back you yell "There is no time to lose!" With a great jump, the dragon lifts off. "How fast are we going?" You ask.

"I'm told we pull 3 G's. That's as if you had two of you stand on top of you while we are speeding up. Hang on!"

With the cool ocean breeze blowing through your hair, you cross the ocean and dive down toward the rainbow dragons' castle. Once safely on the ground, you carefully descend from your mount on the back of your friend and touch the cool moss covered courtyard of the castle.

Suddenly the sun disappears but no stars appear in the sky. You look to your rainbow friend and see that he is bowing toward the ground. Before you can look back toward the sky, you are knocked over by the biggest gust of wind you have ever experienced. Once the wind dies down you look up to stand before the king of the rainbow dragons.

With a booming voice he greets you. "Besty, son of Jacob it is my honour to meet you. My grandfather told me stories of how Jacob blessed us in the design and construction of our castle. It was Jacob who designed the special locking mechanism that keeps our castle safe and stable with these great winds. Do you know how to remove them?"

If you want to go down to the bolts and figure it out once there turn to page 14

If you want to ask the dragon king for help turn to page 17

"I would love to go but we need to discuss this matter with my father." You tell RB. You run inside the castle while your rainbow dragon baths the castle in sunlight reflecting off him.

"Dad, dad, I need your help!" You explain as you find him deep inside the castle in his work shop.

"Haven't I told you to knock?" He asks as his latest project falls to pieces from you startling him.

"Sorry dad, RB just flew in and told me that the rainbow dragons' castle could fall into the ocean at any moment if we don't remove the bolts our great, great, great grandpa Jacob built there."

"And since only a son of Jacob can enter the castle it's up to us?" Your father replies.

"Exactly! Dad, you can fix anything. How can we remove these bolts? How do these things keep a dragon's castle in place with those Norwegian winds blasting it for all these years?"

"Jacob was a great man Besty. He had the dragons build the cliff up over top of an iron base. Then in case such a situation ever came created special release bolts that require a special key to release the castle from its foundation."

"Please tell me you know where this special key is dad."

"Since the castle was designed to last a thousand years, passing a key from generation to generation wasn't practical or safe. Instead on a son's 10th birthday his father is to give him a riddle that only a true son of Jacob can solve."

"A riddle? The rainbow dragon's castle could fall into the ocean to become a modern day Atlantis and all you have is a riddle?" You state as you slap your hand to your forehead. "Alright. Lay it on me."

"You need not search deep in the sand. The key is the tip of your best friend's hand."

If you want to leave now turn to page 21

If you want to solve the riddle first turn to page 26

“Show me the way!” You say as you run into the largest, most beautiful structure you have ever seen. You find it difficult to keep your balance as the earth shudders from the impact of the giant majestic beast running alongside you.

“This way Besty!” RB yells as he squeezes himself through a door way to the left of the main entrance. You run through the same doorway with room to spare. You grab a torch off the wall and are amazed with how rainbows dance off the castle walls from the light reflected off the back of the dragon winding his way through the hallway before you.

"This is as far as I go." RB says once you reach a human sized door. "You'll have to go on by yourself Best."

As you reach for the door, the entire castle rumbles and shakes and you announce "I'm on my way!" Once through the door, you realize that you are beneath the castle. Once your eyes adjust to the darkness, you find yourself starring at four giant bolts locked through huge iron rods that appear to stand right out of the cliff itself.

You make your way to the closest bolt and look for a key lock and are surprised to see the bolt with nothing but a round hole in the center.

“RB. Do you know what key opens this thing up?” You yell back toward the door.

“No. To help us honour our agreement with Jacob, it was decided that only Jacob or one of his sons would have that knowledge.”

If you want to grab an iron bar and try to jab that in the lock turn to page 32

If you want to go back and ask the king of the dragons turn to page 17

"Your majesty, I don't know exactly how to release the bolt. Can you help me?"

"You are welcome to enter our great hall of records." Replies the dragon king. With that he walks so quickly that even running as fast you can RB has to pick you up and has to jog to keep up.

Inside the castle, with only a few torches lit, the great hall is bathed in the most beautiful colours. You realize that the walls are covered in rainbow dragon egg shells and are reflecting the light from just a few light sources.

“What are these?” You ask as you pass by a wall filled with eggs. Some look like rock while others look like giant eggs.

“Besty, rainbow dragons as we are called today are not actually dragons, but like the fearsome Tyrannosaurus Rex, are actually related to ancient birds. Your paleontologists consider us oviraptors.”

“Oviraptors? Like the fossilized egg we have at our castle?” You answer with awe.

“Yes. That fossilized egg is a gift from my grandfather to Jacob to be given along with the key to the first son of each generation of the descendants of Jacob."

"All we have to go with the egg is an ancient raptor claw." You reply. "And how do you possess the ability to speak if you are just a bird?"

"Haven't you ever heard a parrot speak? We're just a little smarter." Answers the king with a smile.

"Wow. I never knew. So you're not a magical creature?"

"Magic? That's funny. No. Alright, here we are." The king reaches over to pull down a giant scroll. “The language they spoke back then here in Norway is Old Norse. Here we have the story of Jacob and the rainbow dragons recorded. Maybe this can help.”

“But I don’t read Old Norse.” You reply.

“Don’t worry Besty, I do. Let’s see… The key is actually given in the form of a riddle that only you, a son of Jacob can answer.

“You need not search deep in the sand. The key is the tip of your best friend’s hand.”

If you can answer the riddle turn to page 34

If you need to get more help turn to page 37

“Dad, let’s go!” You tell your father.

“Besty, I can’t just leave the castle. I have responsibilities to the kingdom and to keep your mother safe. I took an oath on our wedding night to never leave her unprotected. This quest is yours. You are a smart young man with strength beyond your years. Take your bow and arrow and stay close to RB!”

“Thanks dad.” You say with surprise. You have always known this day would come, you just can’t believe it’s already here. Your first quest and it’s to save the home of the rainbow dragons!

“Besty, wait. Before you go there is something else you may need.” Your dad walks out of his workshop and over to the castle’s museum. There he takes out a fossilized raptor egg.

“What do I need this for?” You ask holding the priceless fossil.

“There were two gifts given from the rainbow dragons to Jacob. They might come in handy.”

“Two gifts? I’m holding one egg.” You reply.

"The other is the raptor claw you are wearing around your neck."

"Thanks dad."

"God bless and protect you son."

With that you run to the court yard and mount RB's back and take flight with a great leap.

As you fly across the ocean to Norway, you can't believe how cool and refreshing the ocean air is against your face. You close your eyes for a moment basking in the warmth of the rainbow light as it radiates the sun's warmth on you. Before you know it, you're landing in the great courtyard of the rainbow dragons. Before you is the largest dragon you have ever seen.

RB then introduces you to the king of the rainbow dragons.

"Besty son of Jacob it is my honour to meet you. My grandfather told me stories of how Jacob blessed us in the design and construction of our castle. It was Jacob who designed the special locking mechanism that keeps our castle safe and stable with these great winds. Do you know how to remove them?"

If you can answer the riddle turn to page 34

If you need to get more help turn to page 37

You turn to your father and reply “Dad, what does the riddle mean?”

At that moment, there is a great knocking at the door of your castle. You and your father run to the draw bridge to see RB urgently waving you forward.

“Look!” He says and points into the distant sky.

At first it looks like a cloud of tiny insects flying toward you but in a few minutes you can see it is the entire flock of rainbow dragons.

“Hang on to RB!” Your dad yells as the wind picks up from the flapping of their wings.

Suddenly your courtyard is filled with these ancient beasts.

“What happened?” You ask RB.

“Besty son of Jacob” states the largest rainbow dragon you have ever seen, “I am sorry to say that you and RB took too long to come to our castle. There was a terrible gust of wind and in a moment the entire cliff face slid with our castle into the ocean. We are now homeless.”

You look at RB whose head is hung so low it almost touches the ground.

"Dad, we have to do something."

"What do you suggest son?"

"What about mom's castle? When you were married she left it to start a family here."

At that moment your mother comes running out of the castle to see what all the commotion is.

"Besty, why are all the rainbow dragons in our courtyard?" Your mother asks.

You quickly explain what happened and ask what's happening with the castle she grew up in.

"Why it's being used for tours to students." Your mother answers.

This gives you a great idea and you call the king of the rainbow dragons into an immediate meeting with RB and your parents.

Several days later the headline of the local paper reads "Anastasia's Castle now renamed The Rainbow Dragons' Castle! A local family does right by an old friend. An agreement made generations ago by Jacob and the rainbow dragons has been honoured today. Besty the son of Jacob and his family have donated Anastasia's Castle to the newly homeless rainbow dragons when their castle fell into the ocean in Norway. After significant discussion with local school divisions, the tours of the castle will continue! Now children can meet and interact with real dragons and learn their unique heritage."

You have come to the end of your story, but not the end of the book! Go back again and try a new path to see what other adventures await you in the rainbow dragons' castle!

As you frantically look around to see what you can use to try to pry the lock open, you feel the earth shake and rattle beneath you.

"Hurry Besty! The castle is getting more unstable!" Says RB.

You grab the nearest iron bar and try to jam it into the lock, however the bar is much too round. So you try to place it into the mechanism and try to pry it open.

"Besty, those bolts are holding a CASTLE to the cliff, I don't think I have the leverage to pry it open." RB says.

If you want to try to get RB to get under the castle with you turn to page 38

If you want to go out from under the castle and ask the king of the dragons for help turn to page 17

"RB, show me the way!" You holler as you run into the castle.

"This way Besty!" RB yells as he squeezes himself through a door way to the left of the main entrance. You run through the same doorway with room to spare. You grab a torch off the wall and are amazed with how rainbows dance off the castle walls from the light reflected off the back of the dragon winding his way through the hallway before you.

"This is as far as I go." RB says once you reach a human sized door. "You'll have to go on by yourself Best."

As you reach for the door, the entire castle rumbles and shakes. “I’m on my way!” you exclaim. Once through the door, you see you are beneath the castle and starring at four giant bolts locked through huge iron rods that appear to stand right out of the cliff itself.

You make your way to the nearest bolt and pull out what you think is the key.

If you decide to pull out the ancient key that opens the old storm door at your castle go to page 40

If you decide to pull out your raptor claw necklace go to page 43

“I’m sorry your majesty, but I really don’t know the answer to this riddle. I need to speak to my father. RB let’s go!”

You climb aboard RB and can’t help but notice the worry in the king’s eyes as you lift off.

You can hear the castle creaking as you fly away.

Once across the ocean, you land safely in your courtyard.

“We have to hurry Besty there isn’t much time!” RB says to you

Turn to page 10

"RB, I need you to try!" You run to the door way and use the iron bar to pry the door frame off the wall. "Come on pal! Use those huge claws!"

RB and you rip apart the door frame until the hole is just big enough for the huge beast to crawl through.

Once at the first bolt, the ground begins to shake again. This time it doesn't stop!

"Hurry RB!" You yell as you jab the bar into one of the locking mechanism. "Push!"

RB pushes as hard as he can, but all that happens is the iron bar snaps like a twig.

“Ouch!” RB yells. He pulls his claw back and you can see he hurt his finger nail.

Turn to page 43

The ground shakes harder making it difficult to steady yourself as you reach into your pocket to grab the huge ancient key used in your castle. You find you have to lean against the giant mechanism as you try to place the key in the lock as the ground begins to sink underneath you.

Suddenly the lock is bathed in sunlight and as you try to open the lock you realize the castle's foundation has finally broken.

With a final desperate twist you break the key in the lock with a loud "snap!"

“Besty! We have to leave NOW!” Yells RB. You stumble toward the doorway and struggle to make your way through the corridor as the castle buckles and heaves above you.

You and RB are just able to escape as the castle slides helplessly into the ocean behind you.

Coughing from the dust you look around to see that all the rainbow dragons have broken hearts as they watch helplessly as their home slides away into the depths of the ocean.

“Thank you for trying Besty. You have honoured Jacob’s promise to always help us.” Says the king of the rainbow dragons. “We will all fly you home.”

The flight across the ocean is quiet but not peaceful. You look at the beautiful majestic creatures flying in perfect formation beside you and realize it’s because they are actually giant birds–Oviraptors. Raptors? The fastest bird in the world is a raptor–a falcon!

Once safely in your courtyard, your father comes out of your castle to greet you.

Turn to page 28

The ground continues to shake as your mind races.

"You need not search deep in the sand. The key is the tip of your best friend's hand." The tip of your hand is a finger nail or in the case of a dragon – a claw!

You pull out the ancient raptor claw that was a gift from the rainbow dragons to Jacob and place it in the lock and it snaps open!

"Quick Besty!" Yells RB, "There's not a moment to lose!"

You make your way as quickly as possible to each lock carefully placing the ancient raptor claw into each lock as the castle begins to shift above you.

Once you reach the final lock you look over to see RB bathed in daylight!

“RB the foundation is giving way! Let’s get out of here!”

Both you and RB make your way to the opening forming in the foundation on the north side of the castle. Once outside in the fresh air, you hop on RB and fly to the courtyard.

There you see all the rainbow dragons standing next to giant chains attached to the castle.

RB grabs one and the king of the rainbow dragons hollers "The family of Jacob has kept their promise! Now fly!"

All the dragons lift off in formation like a flock of birds and to your amazement the entire castle slowly lifts off the ground!

After a few moments, the castle is placed safely in a nearby field.

“Where are you going to live now RB?” You ask as you climb down from your friend’s back.

“We don’t know, our goal was to save the castle.” Replies RB

If you want to fly home to discuss the matter with your family turn to page 47

If you feel your quest is complete turn to page 52

"King, you may have your castle, but I would like to help you find a new home."

"What do you suggest Best?" Replies the king.

"Leave some guards here to protect the castle and let's fly to my parent's castle. Maybe there's something we can do to help you find a suitable permanent home." You answer.

Although exhausted from the excitement of the day, you aren't about to let your friends down now when they need you. RB gently picks you up and takes off.

Once home you invite the king of the rainbow dragons and RB into a meeting with your parents to discuss the matter.

"Where would you like to live king?" You ask.

"We have spent past age hiding from mankind. I believe that time is over. Our great hall of records has so much knowledge of the time when our kind – dinosaurs roamed the earth, we could do so much to help your understanding. We have actual feathers from our cousin Tyrannosaurus Rex, ancient unhatched eggs like the one we gave Jacob and so much more."

"Tyrannosaurus Rex was related to a bird? I knew it! They have hollow bones and a giant wishbone!" You explain excitedly! "You don't know how many people have laughed at me for believing that!"

"You were right Besty." The giant dragon says as places his huge talons gently on your head patting you.

"Mom, how much yard space do you have at the castle you grew up at?"

"Lots! In fact, we only use it to give tours for students!" Your mother replies.

Several days later the headline of the local paper reads “Anastasia’s Castle now renamed The Rainbow Dragons’ Castle! A local family does right by an old friend. An agreement made generations ago by Jacob and the rainbow dragons has been honoured today. Besty, the son of Jacob and his family have donated Anastasia’s Castle to the rainbow dragons when their castle was flown in (by dragon) and placed in the giant courtyard. After significant discussion with local school divisions, the tours of the castle will continue! Now children can meet and interact with real dragons and learn their unique heritage."

You have come to the end of your story, but not the end of the book! Go back again and try a new path to see what other adventures await you in the rainbow dragons' castle!

“I’m just glad I could help!” You say and sit down exhausted.

“Let’s get you home.” RB says as he gently picks you up and takes off.

You feel happy you completed your first quest but can’t help feeling uneasy as if there was something else you could have done.

You have come to the end of your story, but not the end of the book! Go back again and try a new path to see what other adventures await you in the rainbow dragons' castle!

www.ingramcontent.com/pod-product-compliance
Ingram Content Group UK Ltd.
Pitfield, Milton Keynes, MK11 3LW, UK
UKHW020216250726
13967UKWH00001B/31

9 781105 332968